COLLETT
The
WONDER VET

Written & Illustrated
by
David Bullock

When Collett was only little, she went for a walk
and met a squirrel.

It was in a tree, in her garden, near the old wooden shed.

And had a large fluffy tail and fur that was red.

The squirrel was sad because its paw was sore, after it leapt and landed upon the prickly floor of a prickly wood, that was just next door.

Collett told the squirrel not to be sad.

Then she ran through the garden to get help
from her dad...

...who opened up a drawer and pulled out a plaster.

And then they ran back, even faster.

They found the squirrel and wrapped its paw and after a week it wasn't sore.

And as she grew older, Collett continued to find
animals, birds and bugs of every kind, to help them
and fix them and make them feel better.

She got a job as a vet, with her name above the door,
so that every single day she could help even more of
the animals, birds and bugs of every kind.

There was a rabbit with bad knees.

There was a mouse, afraid of cheese.

There was a cat who thought he was a hamster...

...and a very angry duck!

There was even a fat poodle who had eaten too
many noodles and got herself stuck inside a tiny
toy truck.

There was a tortoise with an itch...

...and a goose who'd gone giddy.

There was a goat who felt funny.

And a fish called McFiddy.

There was a rooster who had started HOWLING
at the moon!

And an otter who felt hotter than he should do in June.

And to this day Collett continues to care for the animals, birds and bugs everywhere.

So, if you have a frog...

...or a dog...

...or even a cockatoo, and if they're feeling a bit poorly and you don't know what to do.

Just look for the lady whose name is Collett,
who's so kind and so helpful, that they call her...

Wonder Vet!

The End

David Bullock is the author and illustrator of the PC Ben picture book series, which tells the story of a police constable called Ben and the many lives he gets to help every day while out on patrol.

Collett the Wonder Vet is David's fourth children's picture book.

David lives in Hampshire with his family.

Books by David Bullock

You can contact David at wimpresstales@gmail.com.

Printed in Great Britain
by Amazon

85741247R00020